© 1992 Twin Books UK Ltd

Produced by
TWIN BOOKS
Kimbolton House
117A Fulham Road
London SW3 6RL
England

Directed by CND – Muriel Nathan-Deiller
Illustrated by Van Gool-Lefèvre-Loiseaux
Text adapted by Barbara Paulding Thrasher

ISBN: 1-55836-127-8

Printed in Hong Kong

"'VAN GOOL'S'"

Aladdin

TWIN BOOKS

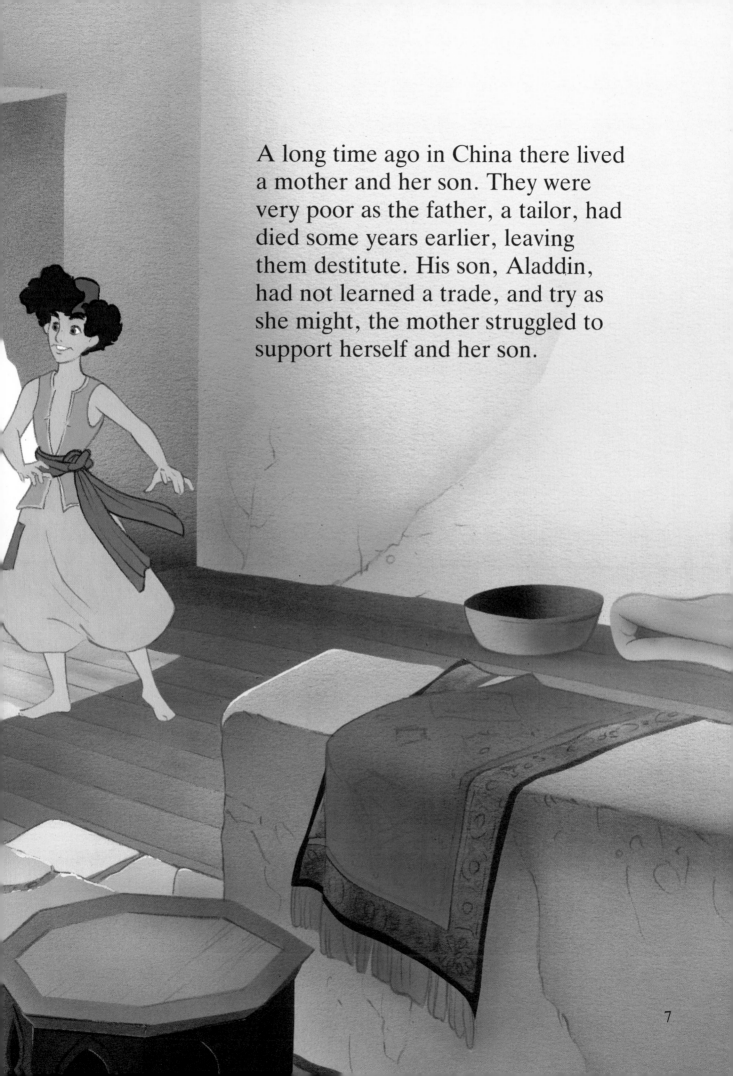

A long time ago in China there lived a mother and her son. They were very poor as the father, a tailor, had died some years earlier, leaving them destitute. His son, Aladdin, had not learned a trade, and try as she might, the mother struggled to support herself and her son.

One day, as Aladdin played in the street, a Magician passed by. He was a crafty man and declared, "My boy! You are the image of my beloved brother. I have been away on business for many years. Take me to your home."

Aladdin's mother was very surprised! "Who are you?" she asked. "My husband has been dead these ten years, and he had no brother!" The Magician looked downcast. "Dear sister, this is indeed sad news. But even if my brother is dead, you and Aladdin are alive. Let's eat and then discuss my nephew's future."

The stranger magically created a sumptuous banquet.

And from that day Aladdin's life
began to change. Elegantly dressed
and well fed by the Magician, he
learned quickly how to do business
with the local merchants.

One evening the Magician suggested to Aladdin that they go for a camel ride. "Saddle up quickly. I want to show you something."

They arrived at a narrow gorge and dismounted.
Aladdin lit a torch and a mysterious flagstone appeared in
front of him.

"Aladdin, move the stone and climb down."

"You will see some beautiful trees with glass fruits on them," coaxed the Magician. "You can take some if you like. But I only want a small oil lamp which you will find at the bottom of the cave. Here, wear this golden ring: it will protect you."

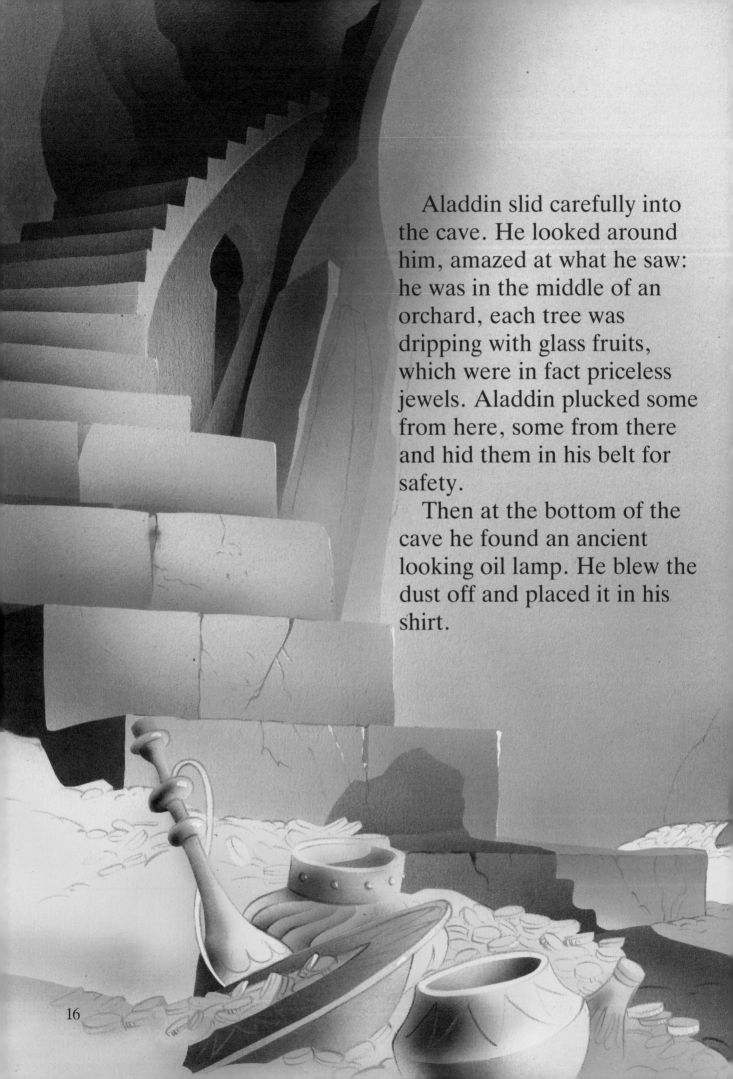

Aladdin slid carefully into the cave. He looked around him, amazed at what he saw: he was in the middle of an orchard, each tree was dripping with glass fruits, which were in fact priceless jewels. Aladdin plucked some from here, some from there and hid them in his belt for safety.

Then at the bottom of the cave he found an ancient looking oil lamp. He blew the dust off and placed it in his shirt.

When Aladdin reached the entrance to the cave he couldn't get out as he was too fat with all the jewels he had hidden in his belt and pockets. "Give me the lamp," demanded the Magician, but Aladdin refused. "No, take my jewels first."

But the Magician threatened, "If you don't give me the lamp I will shut you in the cave forever."

Aladdin didn't want to give in, but suddenly the flagstone closed over the entrance with a thud. His torch went out and he was alone in the dark.

"Uncle, open the cave, please!" But there was no one to hear his cries.

The Magician had left. Aladdin spent two long days in the cave. He was getting desperate. How was he going to get out? He was cold and rubbed his hands to keep warm. A dazzling light flashed, a cloud of smoke billowed about the cave and a genie appeared. "I am the ring's slave, Master, command me and I will obey."

Excited, Aladdin asked the genie to take him home, where he told his mother what the Magician had done. "I knew he was not an honest man," she said.

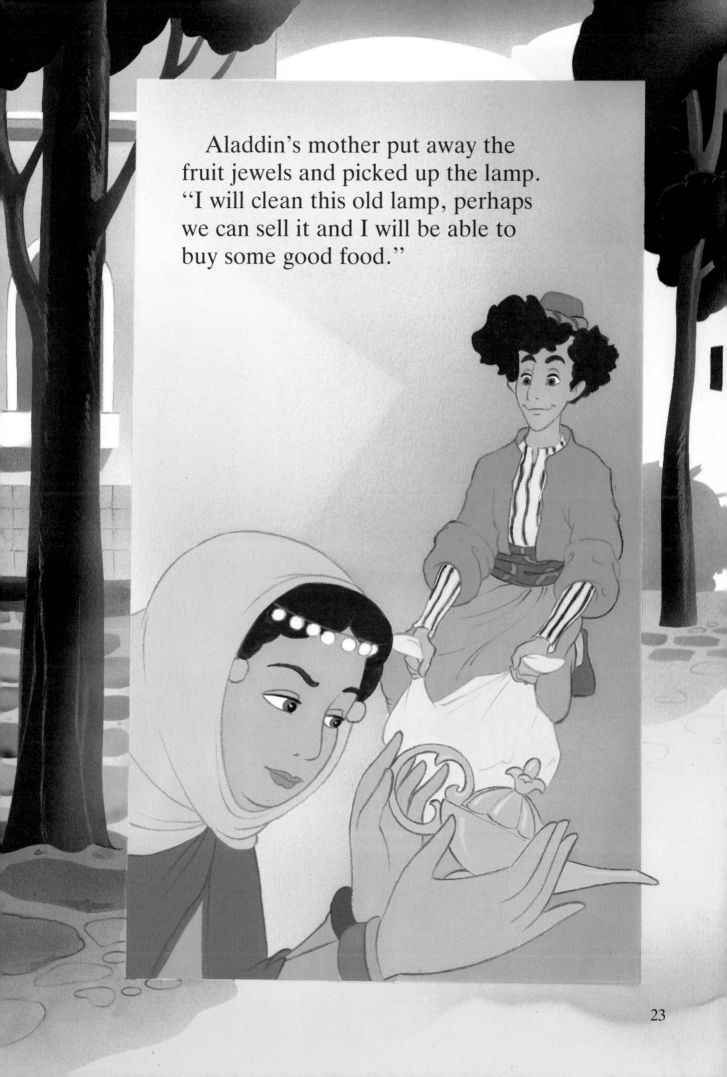

Aladdin's mother put away the fruit jewels and picked up the lamp. "I will clean this old lamp, perhaps we can sell it and I will be able to buy some good food."

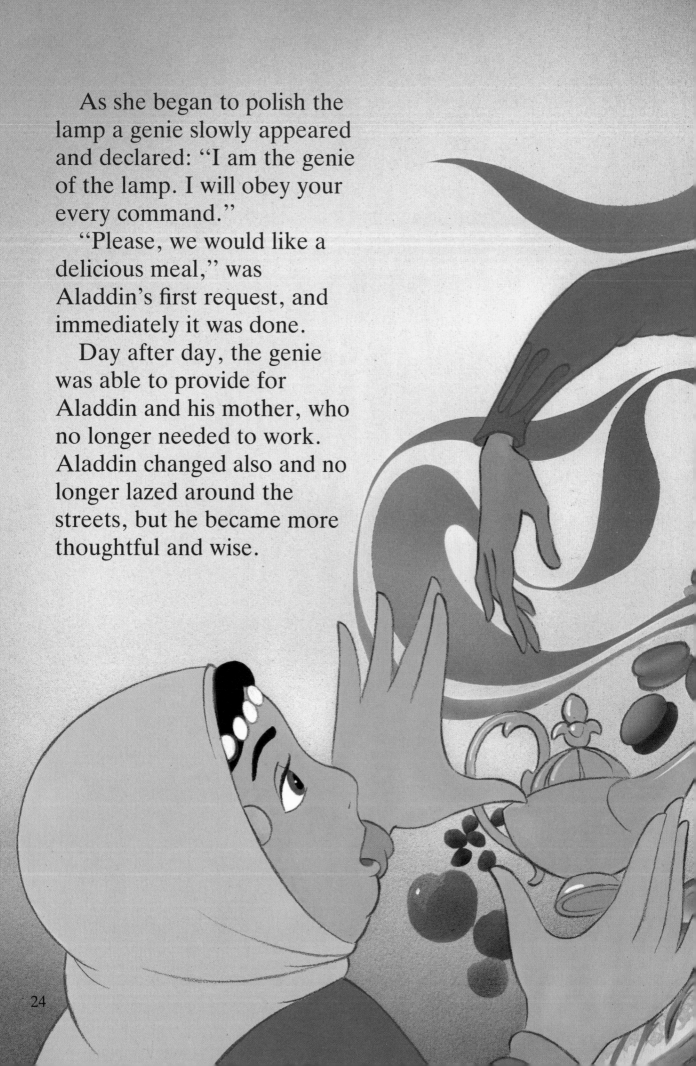

As she began to polish the lamp a genie slowly appeared and declared: "I am the genie of the lamp. I will obey your every command."

"Please, we would like a delicious meal," was Aladdin's first request, and immediately it was done.

Day after day, the genie was able to provide for Aladdin and his mother, who no longer needed to work. Aladdin changed also and no longer lazed around the streets, but he became more thoughtful and wise.

During this time Aladdin grew up; he was a handsome young man now. One day as he was going about his business in the town, the Sultan's daughter and her attendants passed by. The Princess was so beautiful that, even veiled, she made Aladdin's heart beat madly: he would have her for his wife.

Aladdin's mother mocked him when he told her of his desire: "You are but a tailor's son. How can you dare to even look at this beautiful Princess?"

But Aladdin was in love and finally his mother was persuaded to ask the Sultan for Badroulboudour's hand. She prepared the only gift she had; a box full of glass fruits.

The Sultan greatly appreciated the glass fruits, which he identified as priceless gems instantly. Aladdin's mother asked for the hand of Badroulboudour but, alas, the Sultan had already promised her to the son of Vizir. The Sultan did not want Aladdin for his son-in-law but he wanted to keep the jewels, so he announced, "Come back in three months and I will give you my answer."

Aladdin was full of hope, but before the end of the three months he heard of the Princess's wedding to Vizir's son.

Angry and upset, he ordered the genie of the lamp to bring him Badroulboudour.

Immediately the Princess was brought to Aladdin's home. "Don't worry," Aladdin assured her. "I just want to talk with you: I love you and want you to be my wife."

Of course, to begin with the Princess was angry, but after a time she was charmed by Aladdin. She told him, "Go and ask my father for my hand: if he agrees I will obey."

Aladdin summoned the genie of the lamp once more to take the Princess back to her rooms in the palace. Then he ordered: "Prepare forty trays of jewels, and tomorrow morning take them to the Sultan. This time he will give me his daughter!"

35

Next day, on the way to the Sultan's palace Aladdin distributed gold pieces. The people were very happy and thought what a generous young man he was. When the Princess's father saw Aladdin, and all the jewels he said, "I see you are a good man. You may marry my daughter."

That night Aladdin asked the genie to build a palace
for the Princess in front of the Sultan's . . .

. . . and next morning when the people saw it they wondered how it was possible. "It's magic! Long life to Aladdin and our Princess."

A glorious wedding feast was prepared, and the happy couple were married.

In the meantime the Magician (who had pretended to be Aladdin's uncle) decided to make sure that Aladdin was dead in the cave. He conjured up his image and discovered Aladdin was alive, rich, happy and married to the Princess. "Ah!" thought the Magician. "He has discovered the secret of the lamp." The Magician wanted the lamp back, and revenge.

So he travelled to the town where Aladdin lived. He had devised a very clever plan: he went to the palace with new lamps which he proposed to exchange for the old lamps. Everyone laughed at this crazy man.

Aladdin had gone hunting on this particular morning and Badroulboudour, who did not know the value of the magic lamp, saw the Magician through the window. She called to him, and made an exchange, thinking Aladdin would be happy to have a new lamp.

Immediately the Magician rubbed the lamp and the
genie appeared. "I am the genie of the lamp and I will
obey your command."

"Carry this palace and all its inhabitants far away from
this country," ordered the Magician.

The genie blew and in one breath the palace flew over
seas and mountains and arrived in the Magician's land.

The Sultan, noticing that Aladdin's palace had disappeared with his daughter inside, was filled with a great anger. "Find Aladdin!" he ordered his soldiers, "and bring him here." Aladdin tried to defend himself but the Sultan, sure it was all Aladdin's fault, decided to cut his head off. The people were in an uproar. They liked and admired Aladdin, who had been generous to them, and so they demonstrated outside the palace, asking the Sultan for mercy. The Sultan relented and gave Aladdin forty days to find the Princess.

Aladdin was confused and didn't know where to start looking. He was walking by a river thinking, when he suddenly slipped. He tried to keep from falling, and in doing so he turned the ring on his finger. The ring's genie appeared.

Immediately, Aladdin asked him to bring the palace back. But the genie of the lamp was more powerful than the ring's genie. "But I can take you to your wife," suggested the genie.

In an instant Aladdin could kiss his wife again.

"Oh Aladdin, I am so happy to see you," exclaimed the Princess. "This awful Magician wants to take me away from you. Take us home!"

"My darling wife! The Magician is very powerful, the only way to escape is to reclaim the magic lamp."

But this was not going to be easy. The Magician carried
the lamp with him all the time. So Aladdin went to a
market and bought some poison. He showed it to
Badroulboudour, then he hid it in a secret place.

Following Aladdin's instructions, the Princess prepared a delicious meal and invited the Magician for supper.

During the meal the Princess declared: "You're right,
we should marry," and she offered the Magician a glass
of wine . . . with the poison in it. The Magician was so
happy to be stealing Aladdin's beautiful wife he forgot to
be cautious.

He drank deeply from the glass
and slumped dead on to the floor.

Aladdin jumped from his hiding place and took the lamp from the Magician's cloak. He rubbed the lamp and ordered the genie to return them home.

The next morning when the Sultan looked out of his window he found Aladdin's palace in place again. The whole town was yelling with joy. The Sultan was so happy to see his daughter and Aladdin safe again that he ordered a festival, lasting ten days, to celebrate!